Let's Save the
Animals

Frances Barry

CANDLEWICK PRESS

I wish
we could save
all the endangered
animals in the world!

I'd save the
African
elephant,
stomping
across the plains

I'd save the **black rhinoceros,**

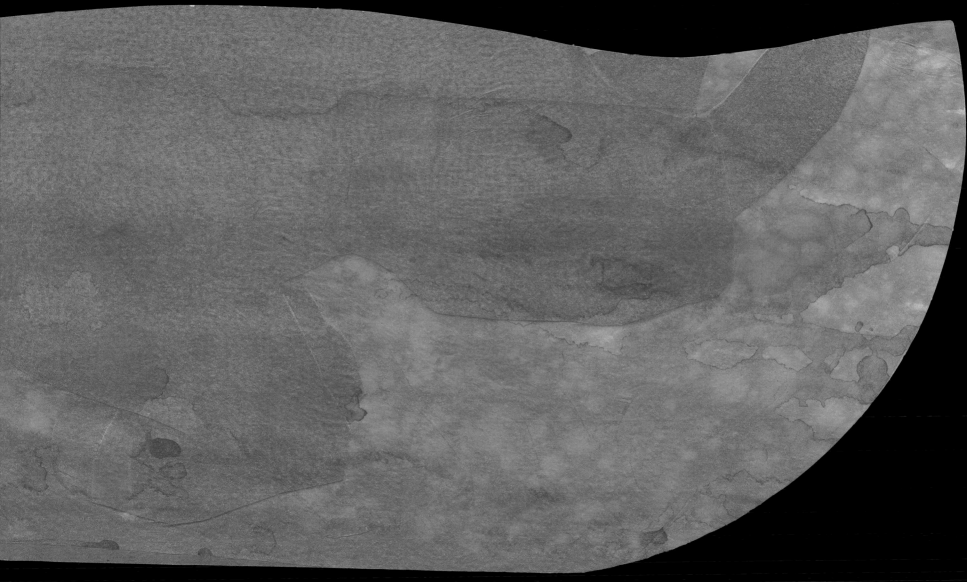

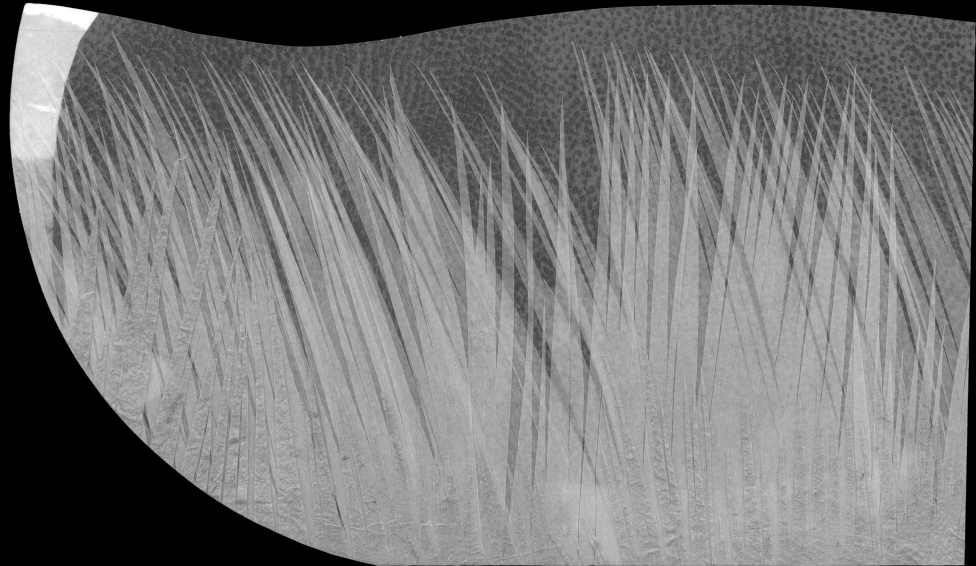

wallowing in a muddy river

and **roaming** through the grasslands.

Black rhinoceroses are poached for their horns, and their homes in
eastern and central Africa are disappearing as people cut down trees.

I'd save the

Amur tiger,

prowling
through
the woods

Amur tigers live in the forests of eastern Russia, which are being cut down. The tigers are also hunted for their skins.

I'd save the **polar bear,**

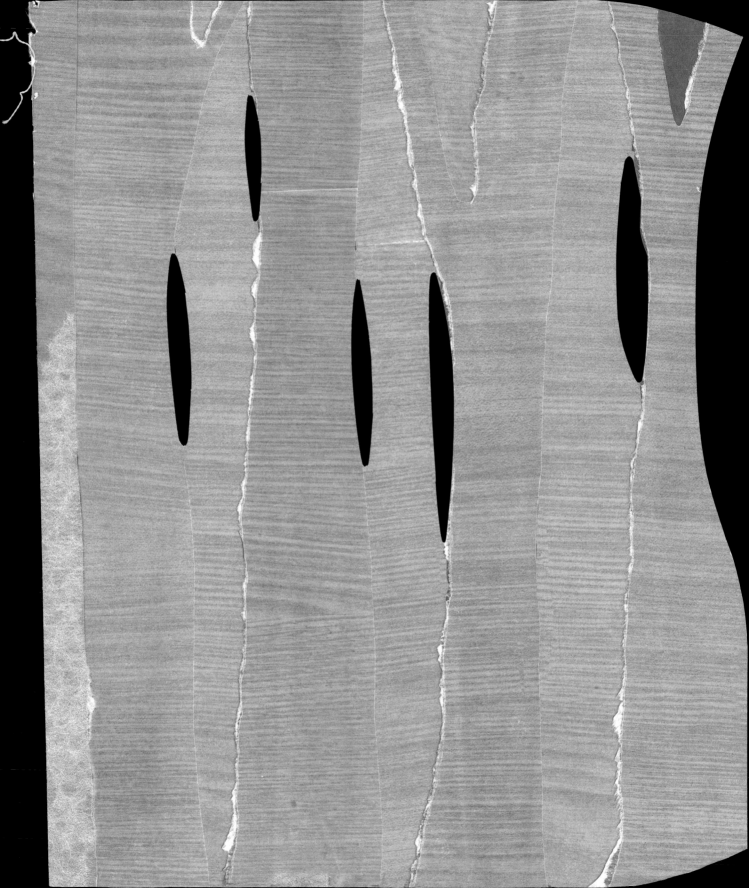

and

pouncing

into a clearing.

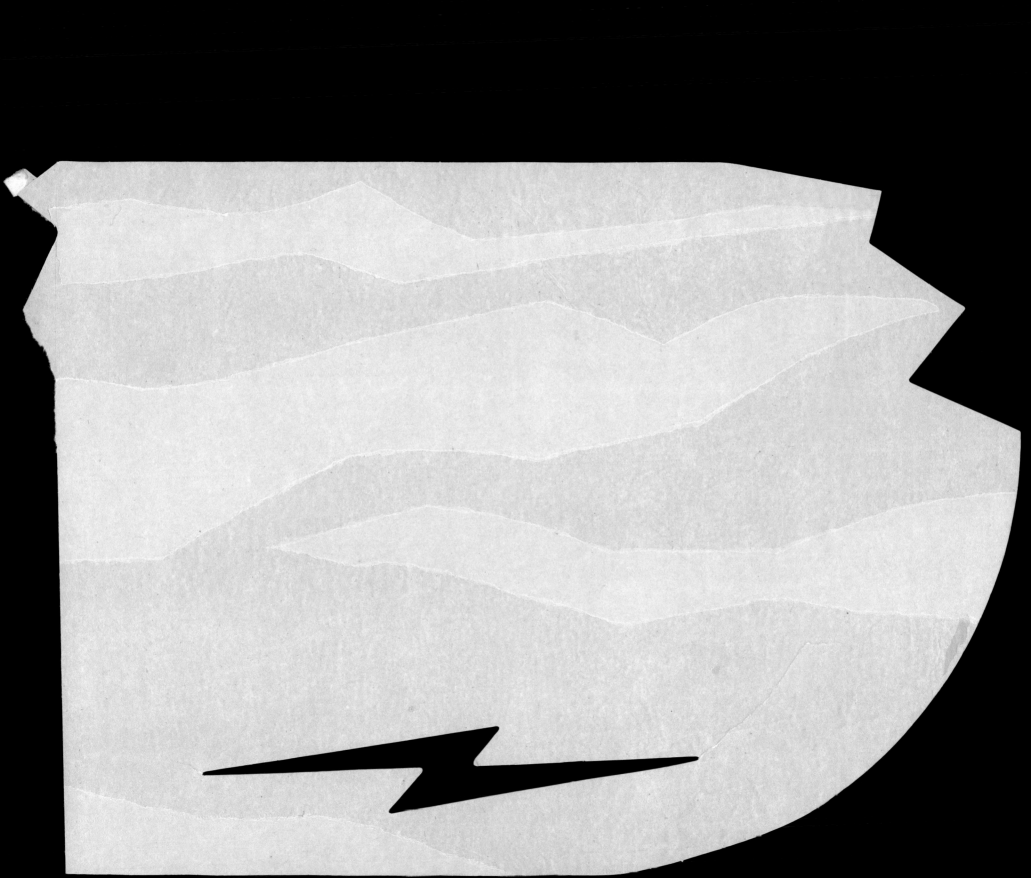

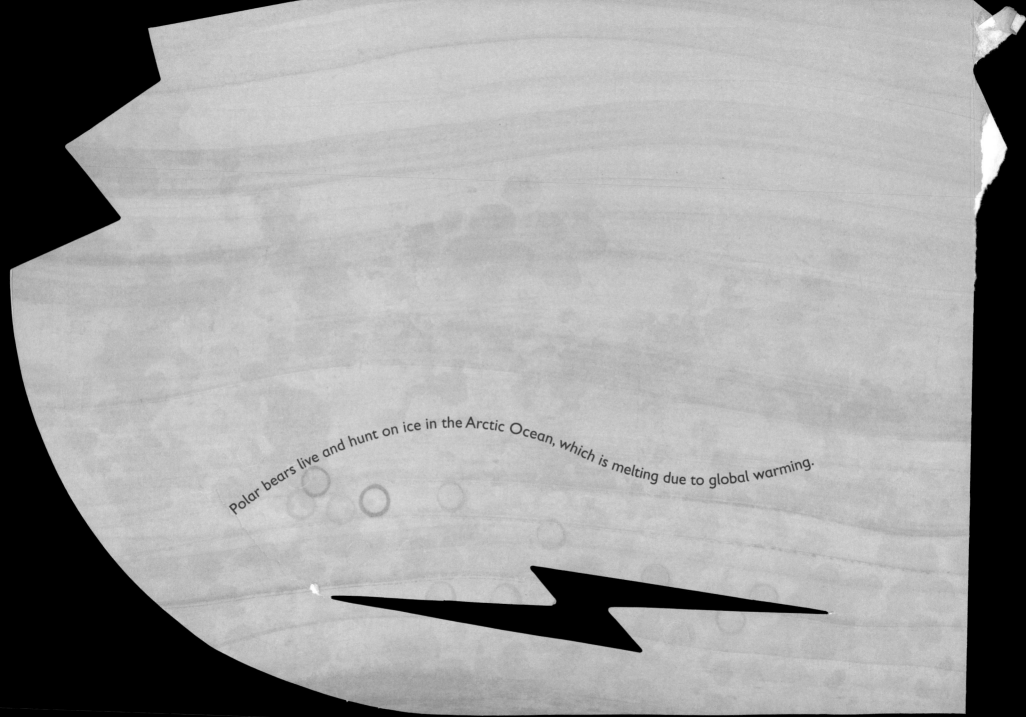

Polar bears live and hunt on ice in the Arctic Ocean, which is melting due to global warming.

strolling across the ice

and **diving** into the Arctic Ocean.

I'd save the
giant panda,
chomping
on bamboo

I'd save the
orangutan,
stretching
from branch to branch

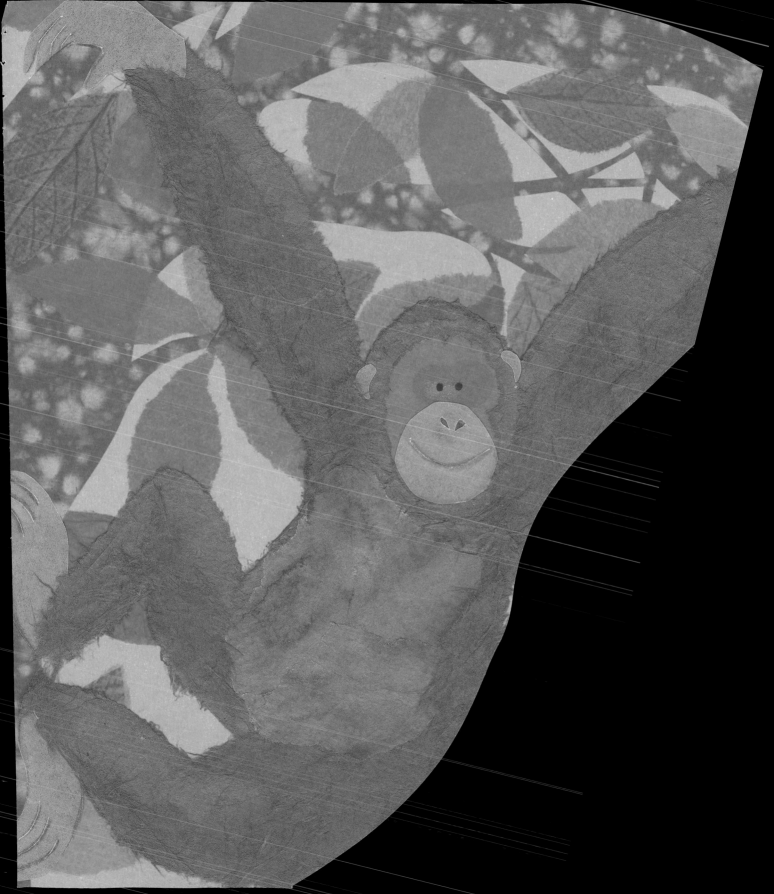

Orangutans' rain-forest homes in Sumatra and Borneo are being cut down for timber and farming.

and swinging

through the tropical rain forest.

I'd save the
Hector's
dolphin,
splashing
through the waves

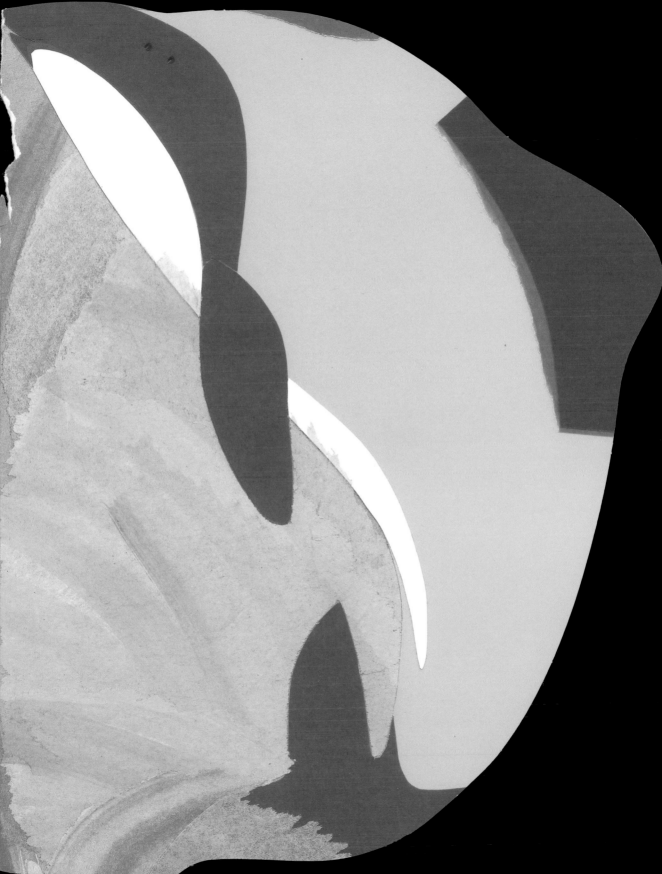

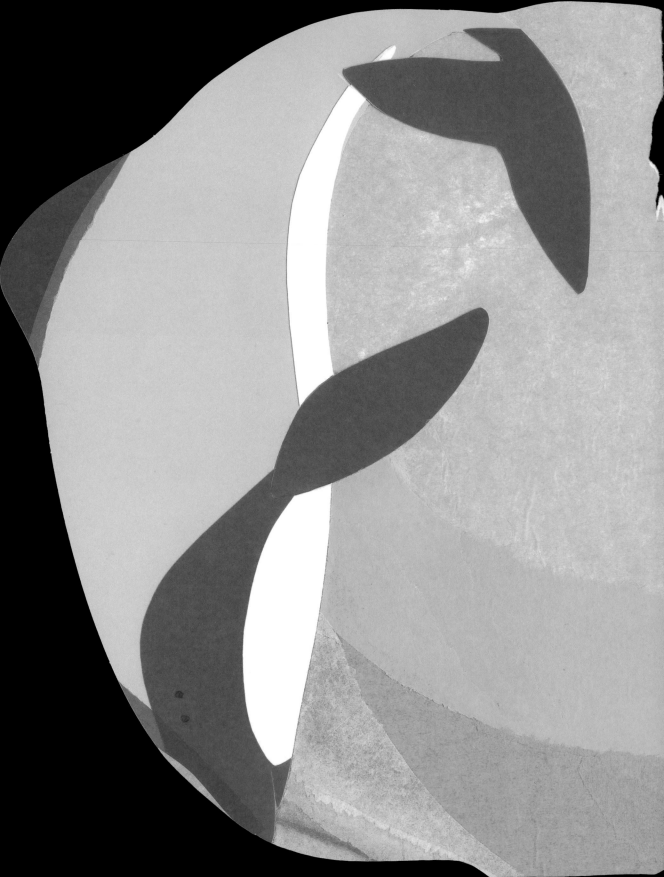

and **surfing** in the sea.

Hector's dolphins live in the sea around New Zealand. They are sometimes accidentally trapped and drowned in fishing nets.

I'd save the
emperor
penguin,
standing
in the snow

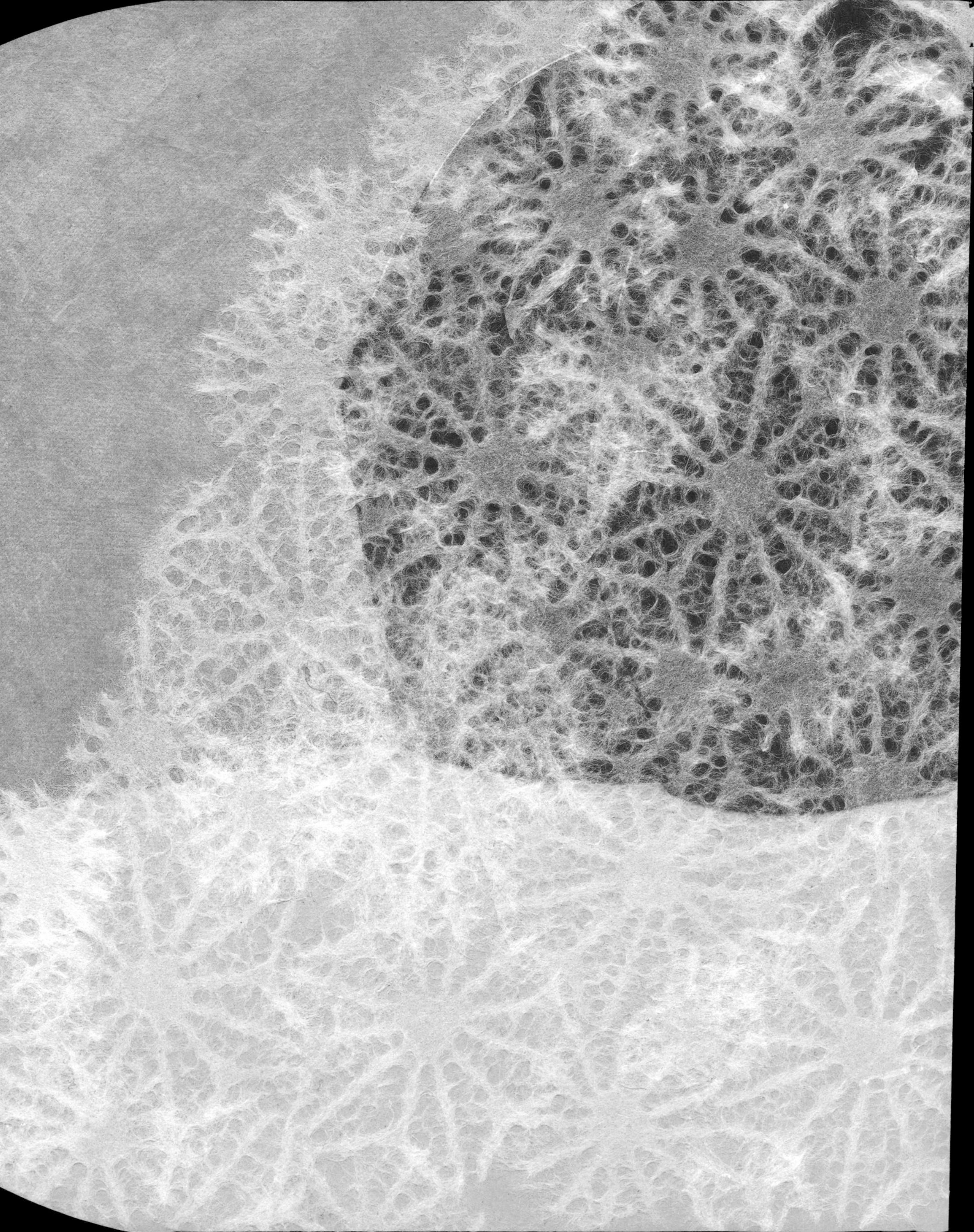

The Antarctic ice, where emperor penguins live, is melting due to global warming.

I'd save the
green turtle,
scuttling across the beach

and skidding across the ice.

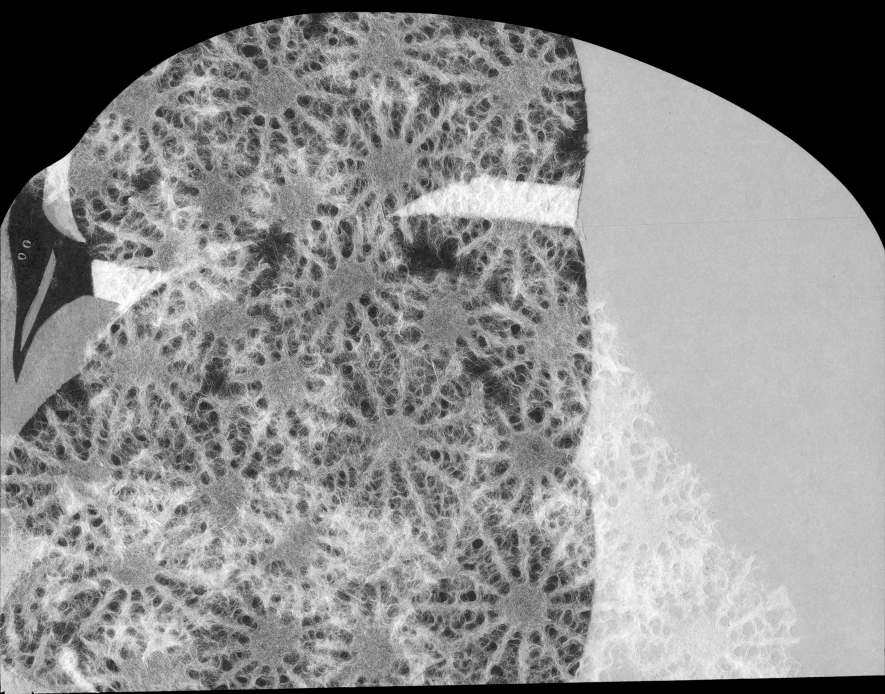

I'd save the
**green
turtle,**
scuttling **across the beach**

The Antarctic ice, where emperor penguins live, is melting due to global warming.

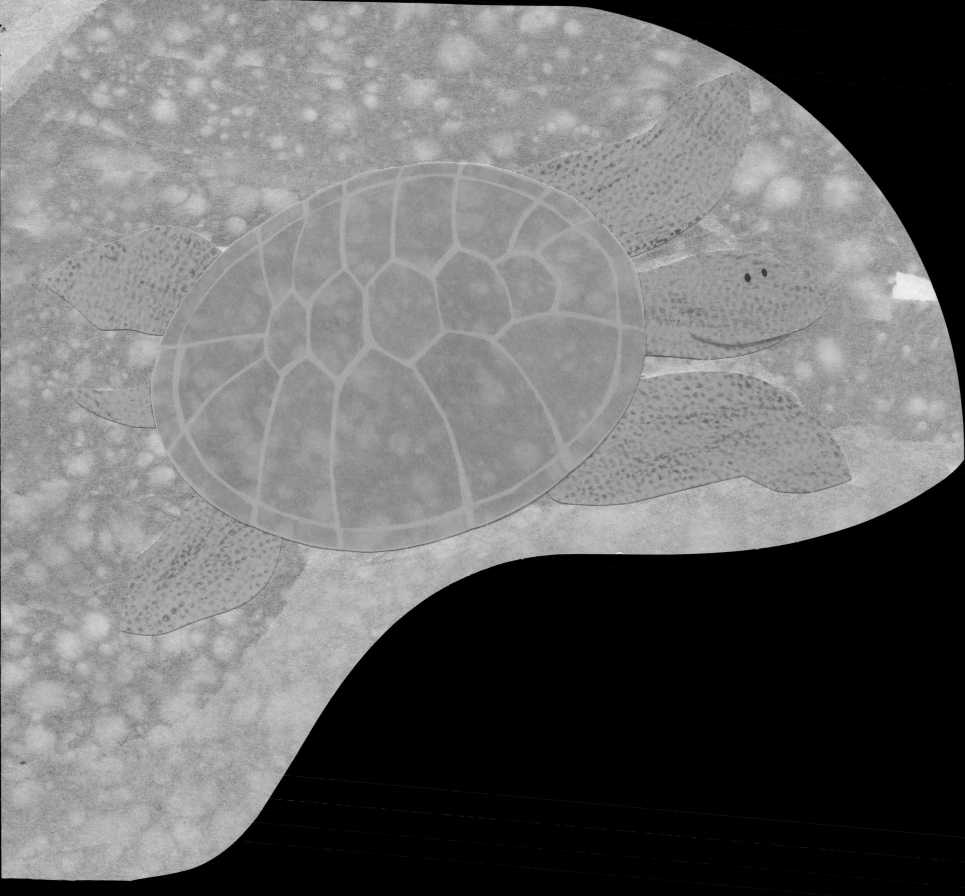

Adult green turtles can get caught in fishing nets and drown.

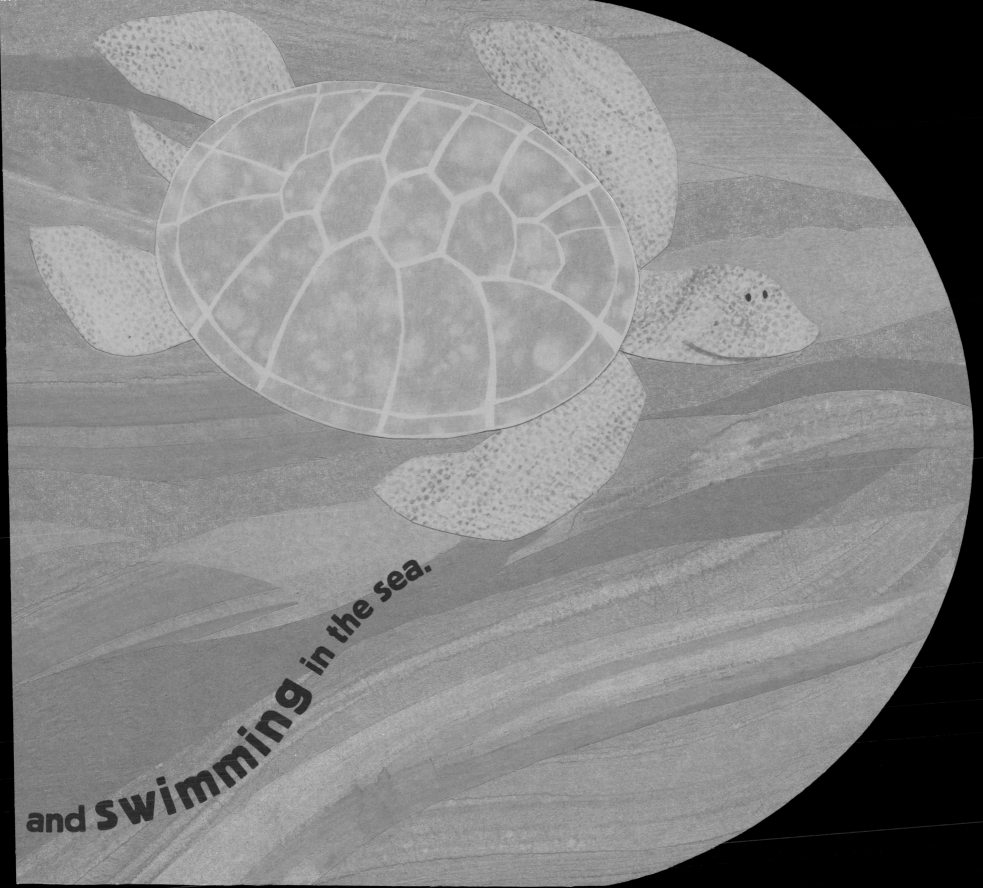

and **swimming** in the sea.

I'd save the **monarch butterfly,**

fluttering in the milkweed meadow.

Monarch butterflies spend summers in North American milkweed meadows, which are under threat from farming and the use of pesticides.

From elephants to ants,

thousands of animals are endangered.

Let's save them all before they are . . .

How can I help?

I can help protect and save the animals with these simple actions:

Adopt an endangered animal
Organize a collection with your class, or ask to sponsor an animal as a birthday present.

Let animals sleep, feed, and play on their own
Disturbing animals in their natural habitats can do more harm than good.

Turn off the lights
Reducing the amount of electricity your family uses can help reduce global warming.

Report sick or injured wild animals to an adult or an animal rescue center
Injured animals need help to survive— but be sure not to touch them!